Richard Scarry's

Things That Go

A GOLDEN BOOK•NEW YORK

Western Publishing Company, Inc.
Racine, Wisconsin 53404

ISBN: 0-307-11817-7/ISBN: 0-307-61817-X (lib. bdg.)

ABCDEFGHIJ

Look at the children make things go.

Huckle throws his paper airplane into the air. It swoops up and down, and all around.

Kitty smacks her hoop with a stick to make it go rolling along.

Babykins leans forward and backward to make the rocking horse go.

Here are some people-powered things that go.
They have to be pushed and pulled to roll along
on their wheels.

Stop, Big Hilda! You can't go
any farther on that bike.
You're much too big for it.

The alarm clock goes tick-tock, rrr-i-i-n-ng. The cuckoo clock goes tick-tock until it reaches four o'clock. Then the bird pops out—cuck-o-o-o!

When Badger blows air through his whistle, it goes bre-e-e-e-t.

The flames go out when Andy blows on his birthday candles. Don't blow so hard, Andy.

The blades of the fan go around and around, and blow air to make the cook feel cool.

Watch out! The cook is making the beater go too fast.

Slow down! The vacuum is going so fast, it's running away with poor Tom.
   Look around your home. How many things that go do you see?

Some of the machines that make new roads have to be big and strong.
The rock crusher goes along, crushing big rocks into small stones.

The asphalt mixer is mixing oil and sand to make asphalt for the surface of the new road.

Stones, tar, and asphalt are spread on the road.
Then the roller goes along, pressing the road flat and smooth.

Look at all the different cars.
They are racing down a mountain road.
Go, cars, go.

Dingo is not such a good driver. He has a problem. Can you see what it is?

Trains go from city to city, carrying big bags
of mail, food, and all kinds of cargo.
    Some people like to go far from home on their vacation.
It's sometimes fun to take a train and not have to drive. But if people
want to take their car on vacation, they can.
It goes on the train's auto carrier.

Water can make things go.
Oh, no! The water is taking Mose
over the edge of the waterfall. Ouch!
Mose, you really should look
where you are going.

The water goes over
the big wheel at the mill
and makes it go around
and around. The big wheel
turns the machinery
inside the mill.

Here are some people-powered boats.
Paddling and rowing make the boats go.
There's something "fishy" about Tom's boat.
Can you see what it is?

There are many different boats in a busy harbor. Some go fast and some go slow. Some have big diesel engines and some have little motors. Some carry people and some carry cargo. The ferry has separate areas to carry people and cars.

At Farmer Pig's farm, the farmhands are busy working with machines. The grain harvester cuts and collects the wheat. The corn picker separates the ears of corn from the stalks. The grass cutter cuts the tall grass for hay. The piglets are having fun riding in the hay wagon.

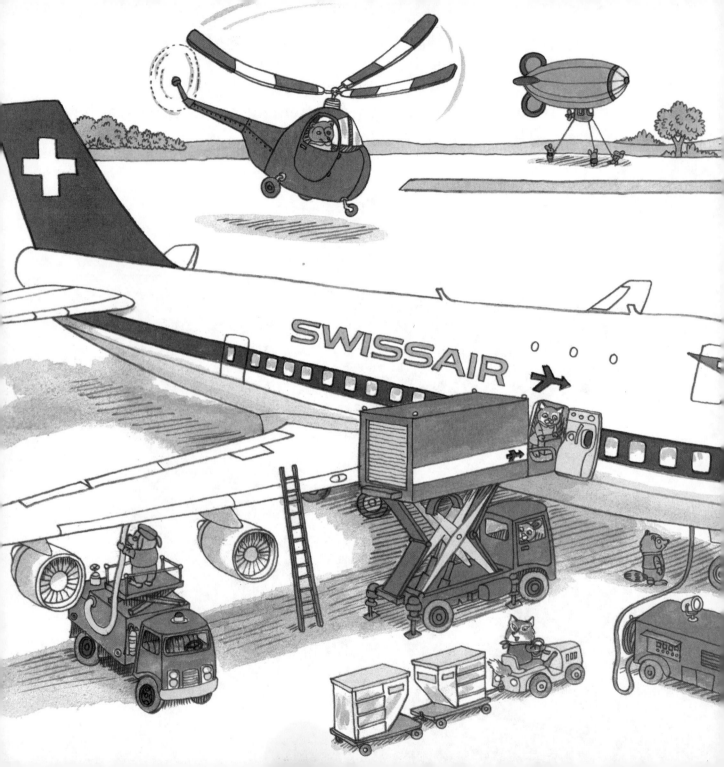

SWISSAIR

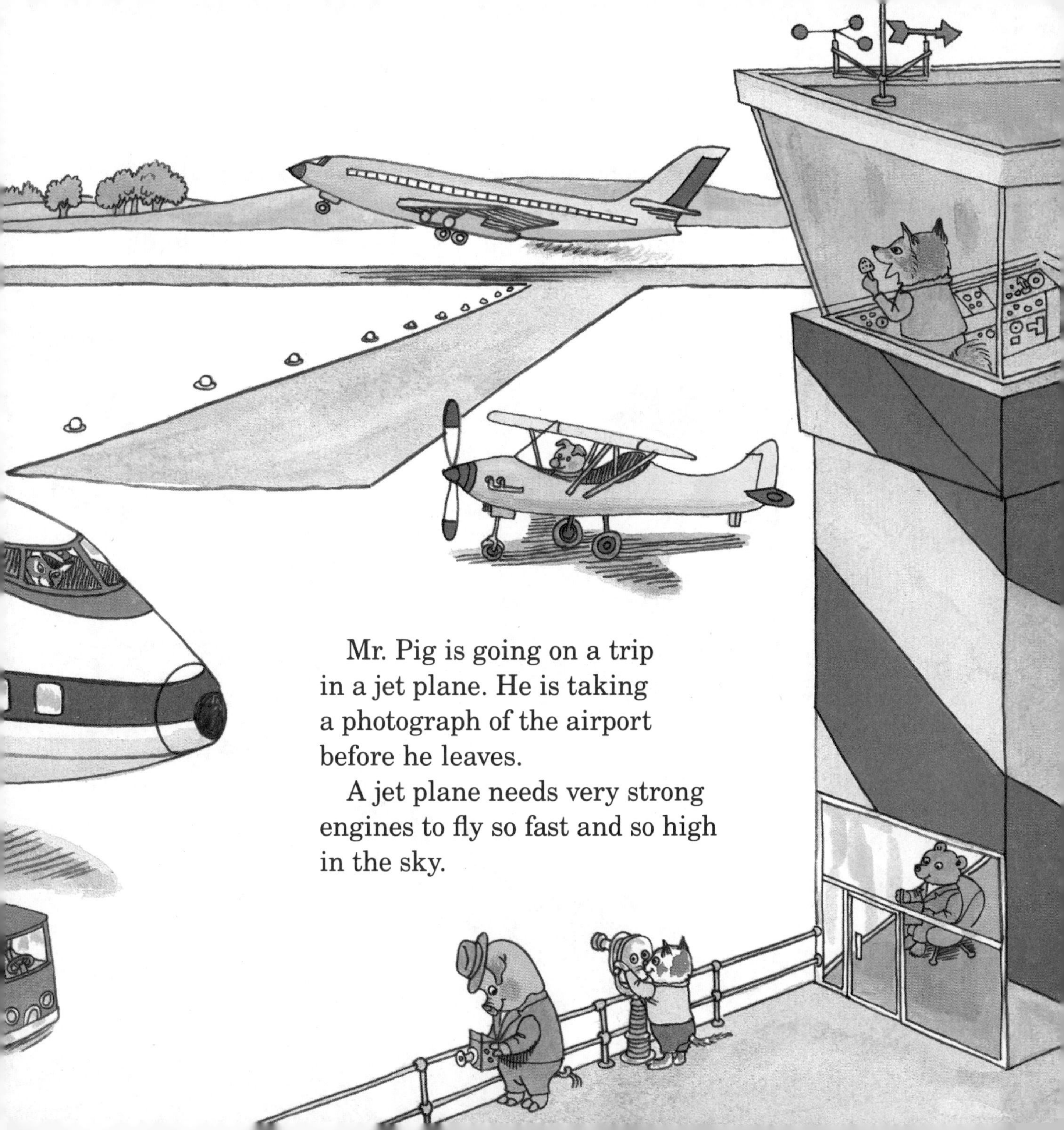

Mr. Pig is going on a trip
in a jet plane. He is taking
a photograph of the airport
before he leaves.

A jet plane needs very strong
engines to fly so fast and so high
in the sky.

The wind can make things go.

Wind blowing on the sails of a sailboat pushes it across the water.

Wind blowing on the blades of a windmill makes them go around. This turns a big wheel, which makes the machinery work inside the windmill.

Hats can sometimes go flying in the wind, too. Hold on tight!

Kitty and Daddy have had such fun learning about all the things that go.

But now it is time for sleepy Kitty to go to bed.

Kitty is going to sleep.
Good night, Kitty.
Sleep tight!